STORM CHILD

Storm Child
Published by Céthial Books for Children
An Imprint of Céthial&Bossche Pro. Inc.
300 Saint Sacrement Suite 307
Montreal, Que. H2Y 1X4

Copyright © 2000 Céthial&Bossche Pro. Inc.
Illustrated by Cathy Alexiou and Jean-Marc Bock.

First Edition
10 9 8 7 6 5 4 3 2 1
ISBN: 1-894155-01-7
Library of Congress Catalog Card Number:
National Library of Canada

Distributed by Céthial&Bossche Consumer Products

Phone: 1-888-265-2479
Email: cethial@cethial.com
Cethial On Line: www.cethial.com

To Anita and Sophie.

STORM CHILD

Keith Cavele

Illustrations by Cathy Alexiou
and Jean-Marc Bock

Cèthial

Storm Child,
Between clouds and rain
Yearning for love
In the eye of a hurricane.

FRIDAY

SOPHIE LIVED WITH HER FATHER in Silver Mine Bay, in an old hotel on the edge of the Southern Sea. Once the town had been the very center of a breathless new age, but now, in the closing years of the twenty-first century, it lay silent, alone in the winter wind and rain and in the summer heat. The seam of pure silver that had given the town its name had run out long ago, and with it the prosperity that was now just a memory.

Sophie was only eleven years old, too young to remember how things had once been. Long ago, people had come from far away to marvel at the extraordinary revolving bandstand, at the long pier with its great Pleasure Dome, at the holographic clock tower that changed colors with the seasons. For Sophie these things were nothing but relics, the ghosts of memories she was sure she would never share.

The fortunes of her father, Joe, had followed those of the town. In the days of prosperity, his father had built the magnificent West Bay Hotel. As a young man Joe had been handsome, like his father. He met and soon married a beautiful young woman whose name was Sylvia. She was a ballerina, a soloist with the Silver Mine Bay Ballet until Joe had swept her off her feet and into the dance of life.

However, like most of the townspeople, they saw their parents' prosperity pass them by. By the time they decided to have a child, they were no longer young. Sylvia died when Sophie was born. Her mother's death was a mystery her father would never talk about.

Joe was left alone with the infant Sophie and with his grief. A great sadness settled on him that weighed down on his shoulders. Gone was the infectious sense of humor that had won a ballerina's heart.

His sadness was much like the town's. With the silver spent, people no longer had a reason for coming to Silver Mine Bay, much less stay in a luxury hotel. It became a lonesome, empty place. Joe would spend his days and nights with his cronies, reminiscing about the glorious past. He forgot about the outside world, forgot about his daughter.

Her father's remoteness hurt Sophie, but being alone gradually became part of her everyday life. She never knew the simple joys of a normal childhood, like her playmates and school friends had. Her home was an empty, echoing hotel, and her companionship was herself and her father's silent remorse.

She spent so much time alone that she built her own world around her, a world of imagination and dreams. In fact the more she dreamed, the richer and more colorful and satisfying her dreams became. Many of them involved the Pleasure Dome at the end of the pier. She could see it from the window of her bedroom in the hotel, shining in the sunlight or gleaming in the glow of the moon. Time and again she had asked her father to tell her its story; time and again he refused. He would cough and turn his head away, or hurry downstairs to do some chores.

By the fifth grade Sophie had become almost an outsider at school. It saddened her teachers to see her trudging home along the sea-front promenade each day, like a solitary waif, but the warmth of her smile and the joy a simple "Good morning" would bring to her eyes quickly convinced them she was not unhappy.

And it was true. Inside her burned a fire, a spirit that was already beyond her control. Even though she could not understand what it was, she felt its power growing, urging her on.

On this day, as she was making her way home from school around the great arc of the bay, a strong wind sprang out of a metallic gray sky. Quickly it gathered strength, becoming so powerful that she had to lean into it as she struggled along the deserted promenade.

Wiping her streaming eyes on her sleeve, she looked at the ocean and the sky. Waves were already pounding against the old sea wall and the spray, like the dust of thousands of white horses, whipped toward her, driven by the gale, soaking her face and hair. She could hear the frantic clanging of the bell on the mooring buoy out in the bay.

This was going to be a bad storm, maybe even a hurricane. Head bent low, Sophie fought her way ahead. The wind was growing stronger by the minute. The awnings on the buildings fronting the ocean were snapping so violently it seemed at any second they might lift into the air and blow out over the bay. The few palm trees that still remained along the promenade were bent low, their scraggly fronds almost brushing the ground. In the distance, a cloud of wind-driven spray hid the pier.

In spite of the danger, Sophie suddenly knew she was not afraid. The power of the growing storm called out to her. Her heart stirred. Her spirits soared. She wanted to stretch her arms wide and let the great wind carry her away, swerving and dipping and swooping with the gulls over the roaring waves.

When Sophie finally reached the steps in front of the West Bay Hotel, she saw that the wind had ripped two heavy wooden shutters from the wall. A third was hanging by a single hinge and smashing into a window frame. Rain was pouring into the dark hallway through the broken glass. Sophie slipped inside. The front door closed behind her with a bang. For an instant she stood motionless, listening to the sounds outside, the voices of the wind.

Suddenly she heard another voice. A harsh, rasping laugh was coming from the room beyond the main stairway. It used to be a sailors' bar known as The Snug. It had been closed for years, but she knew her father used it for meeting his pals, aimless men like himself.

Taking off her soaking coat and scarf, Sophie was about to investigate when she heard the sudden crash of glass breaking on the wooden floor, followed by muttered curses. Seconds later, the door to the bar flew open. Her father stumbled across the corridor into the lounge on the other side. Almost immediately he returned, a bottle of whiskey in his hand.

He was unshaven, and his clothes were rumpled as though he had been struck by the hurricane raging outside. He entered The Snug, slamming the door shut behind him. He didn't even notice Sophie standing a few feet away in the corridor.

She went up to the closed door and stopped for an instant. Should she go in, or not? Would her father be angry with her? Behind her in the hallway, the broken shutter continued to flail against the window frame. Just as she was about to open the door, a gust of wind swept down the hall and blew it wide open.

Seamus O'Sullivan, who had been a building contractor back when there were things to build in Silver Mine Bay, lost his balance and with a thud fell off his stool, landing on the floor. Besides her father, two other men were seated at the bar, surrounded by a smoky blue haze. One was Tom Valentine, a sly tailor for whom there were no longer customers, the other was Chester Parks, the band leader whose orchestra once had entertained summer strollers in the bandstand beside the pier.

They were yesterday's men, drinking to forget the past as they retold the events that had brought them together, during this storm, in a derelict town on the edge of the Southern Sea.

As always, the talk had turned to silver, that gleaming metal which was still a greedy obsession with these men. Silver: that was what kept them going. They dreamed that perhaps tomorrow one of them might discover an untapped seam, the prize that would bring them wealth, and bring the town back to life.

Sophie stood motionless for a moment, blinking from the smoke.

Then her father's voice boomed out, "Well, well, look what the wind blew in."

"Dad, one of the shutters broke the window in the hall. The rain's blowing through and . . ."

Seamus O'Sullivan, who had picked himself up off the floor and climbed back onto his stool, interrupted her with a chortle.

"Hey, Joe, better attend to it real snappy now, before your guests complain!" Her father grunted, reached for the

The fortune of her father, Joe, had followed those of the town.
In the days of prosperity, his father had built the magnificent West Bay Hotel.

bottle of whiskey, poured himself a drink, then trudged through the door and down the hall toward the clattering shutter, as though walking in his sleep.

As he went past her, Sophie turned her head aside. Would he remember that tomorrow was her birthday?

Sophie went up the creaking stairs to her bedroom. Snuggling under the covers, she pulled herself up onto her pillow so she could peek out of the window. Over the horizon rushed clouds, darker and more threatening than any she'd ever seen before. Her window rattled as the wind grew even stronger. As the waves raced up the beach, it was almost as if she could taste the salt spray on her lips.

Powerful emotions poured over Sophie like the onrushing surf. There was something familiar about all of this . . . but what? She wanted nothing so much as to run down to the water's edge. The ocean and the sky seemed to be calling out to her. Suddenly, she knew what they were saying.

It was hope, carried by the wind, hope that swept through the hallway below, that blew fresh and strong through the emptiness of the old hotel.

Night was falling as the wind howled and the building creaked and trembled and swayed, yet held firm, for it had been built to give with the hurricanes that blew in from the Southern Sea in late summer. Then, as she looked toward the pier, Sophie saw a flickering light. That was impossible. Nobody ever went there, especially at the peak of a hurricane.

She rubbed her eyes, and looked again. The light was gone. Often, if she stared at the ocean long enough, she would see shapes beneath the waves, mysterious shadows, things glinting from below, reflecting the rays of the sun. Maybe that was what Sophie had seen blinking from the tip of the pier, but the light was not a shape beneath the water; she had seen it. And the light had seemed to be beckoning to her, like a beacon in the storm. Then she fell asleep.

Sophie must have slept for some time. It was completely dark in her room when she awoke, roused not by the roar of the wind, but by another sound that had reached into her dreams and pulled her back into the world. Wiping the mist from the window with her hand, she peered outside. The porch lights were on below, transforming the rain into silver threads.

She got dressed and rushed downstairs, grabbed a yellow raincoat from the hall closet, and hurried toward the front door, her feet splashing in the puddles on the floor. There, silhouetted against the driving rain, stood her father, fists clenched at his sides, his head held high. She could hear him shouting at the storm. The wind whipped his voice away before she could grasp them fully. Then she heard three words distinctly:

"You killed her!"

All at once, she understood. Her mother had died in the great hurricane that hit Silver Mine Bay twelve years before as Sophie was being born. She was the child of the storm that had killed her mother.

Sophie struggled across the porch against the full force of the gale. Finally she reached his side, and reached out her hand toward his. At her touch he looked down, his face drenched from the rain, lightly brushed her head with his right hand, then turned abruptly and rushed back into the hotel.

How fast
Time's arrow finds
That spot in her heart
Where destiny unwinds.

SATURDAY

BY DAYBREAK THE HURRICANE had blown itself out. Sophie's late-night encounter with her father seemed as far away as a bad dream. It was Saturday; she could spend the whole morning searching for treasure washed ashore during the storm.

Sophie jumped out of bed and got into her beach clothes as quickly as she could. Downstairs, she found her father sound asleep on a couch in the hotel office. Tenderly, she placed a cushion under his head and left him to sleep. The floor of the entrance hall was littered with broken glass lying in the puddles. Quickly she swept it up and rushed outside.

A light breeze was blowing. The air was clear and fresh. The rising sun was already turning both the sea and the sky a richer shade of blue; its warming rays sparkled on the waves. Sophie took one huge, deep breath, holding it in until she started to feel dizzy. Then she released it with a gasp and ran down the beach to where the surf came frothing to meet her like a friend.

Spinning in the sand, she saw how the wind and waves had driven debris onto the promenade. Whatever the wind had ripped from the buildings along the sea front lay strewn about along with felled palms, their stumps now wrapped in bandages of kelp.

She could see the Pleasure Dome from the window of her bedroom.

The bright sun couldn't hide the terrible beating the town had taken. At least a dozen beach gliders lay in pieces, far beyond repair. Silver Mine Bay had always been proud of its beach gliders, self-propelled armchairs with handlebars. They had been invented right here, by a man named Mystic Jack. In the old days they used to glide bathers between the promenade and the beach. Sophie had always wanted to try one, but she was too young. "When you grow up," her father once told her in a light-hearted moment, "maybe we'll take a beach glider to visit Mystic Jack." And he had given her one of his rare smiles and winked.

She started walking toward the pier. Stooping to pick up a piece of driftwood, she spotted a plume of spray a few hundred yards off shore. It was a surfacing whale! She waited, keeping her eyes glued to the spot. Soon the creature's huge tail rose high above the surface. Then slowly it disappeared beneath the rolling waves. Though she had heard stories of how whales used to visit the bay, this was the very first time she had seen one. What a wonderful birthday present!

Finally, Sophie reached the wooden carcass of an old longboat that had long ago washed up on the sand. It was a favorite refuge of hers, a fine place to rest and to daydream. She loved its ancient timbers, worn so smooth and white, washed by the ocean and scorched by the sun for more years than she could imagine.

As she lay there lost in her thoughts, she suddenly saw another unusual sight. A thin column of smoke was rising from a spot up on the pier. It seemed to be coming from the Pleasure Dome, the same place she had seen the light the night before.

Warning signs were posted on the beach. The whole structure was dangerous, off limits to all citizens, the signs proclaimed in big red letters, but the smoke had awakened her curiosity. Shading her eyes, Sophie searched for signs of life, but everything seemed silent, deserted. Only the waves rose and fell among the tangled iron supports that bore the weight of the mighty Pleasure Dome.

She had overheard her father's friends talk about a magic orchestra that played on soft summer nights. How could there be an orchestra if no one lived there?

Sophie looked out toward the tip of the pier while her imagination took wing. The years had blended the pier's original brilliant colors into softer shades of blue and orange that reflected the sun like glass, a mirror of the ocean and the dawn sky. In front of the Pleasure Dome, closer to the shore, stood the red-white-and-blue tower of the tallest, longest, fastest water slide in all the Southern Sea. Sophie had been born too late to try it, but she remembered the old advertisements in the tourist guides now gathering dust in the West Bay Hotel.

Fifty yards from the slide, the pier came to an abrupt end. Jagged metal, hung with large clumps of kelp, entwined with lengths of cable dangled close to the surface of the water. Up on the promenade old turnstiles, a big arch, and a ticket booth marked the pier's original end point. The missing section had broken off twelve years ago in the Great Storm of '83, making the pier inaccessible except by boat. In fact, it was like a man-made island just off shore.

Sophie noticed the tide's going out. If she waited, it would soon be low tide. She felt an overwhelming urge to find out what mysteries, what secrets lurked out there, in the great Dome. She yearned to find the light that had winked at her last night at the darkest hour of the hurricane.

She had to get onto the pier! After all, she was twelve years old today! Wading out in the sea water that came above her knees, she soon spotted a metal ladder that extended right into the water. Now if only the tide would go out just a little bit more, she would be able to reach it.

She returned to the old hull and lay down to wait. She watched the sun climb slowly in the sky. Its warmth and the sea breeze must have made her sleepy; soon she found her eyelids growing heavy.

Perhaps an hour had passed when suddenly a loud

squawking awakened her. A seagull perched just above her head was telling her it was low tide at last. In fact, it was the lowest of low tides that followed a storm. The metal ladder was completely out of the water.

Picking her way through the kelp and the clams in the shallows, Sophie reached out and took hold of the ladder. How slippery it was! She had to be careful not to lose her footing. Cautiously, she hauled herself up until she was able to get a toe hold on the bottom rung. The metal was cold on her feet, and for a second or two she wondered whether this was such a good idea after all, but she looked up through the planking of the pier toward the gleaming Pleasure Dome, and thought of all the hidden treasures it might conceal. Her excitement gave her strength and confidence to go on. Two steps more, and she climbed out onto the wide deck. Sophie ran toward the remains of an ice-cream stand. Ahead of her towered the Pleasure Dome. Close up, it was really huge. Sophie was frightened and thrilled at the same time. Not wasting a moment, she hurried toward the big doors.

She expected to find them locked, but they swung open before her. Suddenly she was inside. The silence was eerie. Straightening her clothes, she peered into the shadows. Narrow beams of light filtered down from small holes in the big curved ceiling high above.

The wind was growing stronger and the spray soaking her face and hair.

Sophie's heart was pounding with excitement as she walked slowly down the center aisle, past rows of deep-red velvet-plush seats. A breath of wind from outside sounded like the collective sigh from the ghosts of the audience that had once packed the hall.

Then it happened! Sophie froze right where she stood. With heart-hammering suddenness, the great hall was filled with music so beautiful that her feelings soared. She sat down and found herself dreaming of mountains, of great fir trees laden with snow, of majestic glaciers reflecting the sun like glass. A clash of cymbals made her eyes dart upward. She saw huge chandeliers made of solid ice sparkling in the frigid air that enveloped the hall.

Fluffy snowflakes started to drift down. Sophie clapped her hands with joy. A golden sun rose from behind the wide empty stage. As the shadows vanished, Sophie saw the orchestra pit begin to rise, while the snow fell in fat, gentle flakes. An entire orchestra was playing. And in its midst, a huge organ pulsated with bright rainbow colors. A puff of wind blew away the snow that covered the front of the stage, and dancers, at least a hundred of them, swept out onto a sheet of ice. They swirled and waltzed in a glittering array. Then a bell rang.

Suddenly, the sun went dark, the snow ceased, the dancers and the orchestra disappeared. Now only the organ stood alone on the dark stage. At its keyboard sat a man in a black tailcoat. The music he played sounded like the voice of a child, so serene that tears came to Sophie's eyes. She blinked and in that second the entire dome was filled with stars.

The music grew softer, and slowly the organ sank below the stage until, except for the whisper of the breeze outside, everything was silent.

Suddenly Sophie felt a light tap upon her shoulder. She jumped, turned in her seat, and came face to face with a strange looking man with the bluest eyes she ever saw. She recognized him at once as the organist in the black tailcoat. He smiled at her. She smiled back, because in that instant, something told her she had met a friend.

"Hello, I'm Jack," he said in a warm voice. She reached out her hand to shake his. "I'm Sophie," she said with a smile. Glancing briefly back at the dark empty stage, then up again at the great curve of the dome, she returned her eyes to his still smiling face. Could this be the same man her father had told her about long ago?

"How did you do all that?" she asked. Jack's eyes lit up. "Well, Sophie, I wish I could say it was magic, but in truth it was only technology. Now, come with me," he said, jumping to his feet. "And I'll show you."

Sophie got up and followed Jack over to the side of the

stage. He opened a hidden door, which led down to the orchestra pit below. All the instruments were still laid out. Brass horns gleamed on their stands – trumpets, trombones, and two big fat tubas. Then there were the violins arranged neatly in three rows. Next to them the woodwind and percussion instruments, marimbas, guitars, a xylophone, and, of course, the great organ. Only the musicians were absent.

On the seat of each chair, however, Sophie noticed a luminous area that glowed in the semi-darkness. She reached out for a trumpet, but gasped in surprise when her fingers closed on nothing but air. She moved both her hands around where the instruments seemed to be but found only empty space.

Baffled, she looked at Jack. Without a word he pointed high overhead, where Sophie now saw pinpoints of light shining downward to focus on the spot where each instrument appeared to be.

"Watch this," Jack said, grinning. He sat down at the organ and began pulling out the stops. The whole orchestra pit began to rise. Cautiously, Sophie stretched out her hand towards the organ, fully expecting to find more empty space. Instead her hand connected with the dark polished wood that surrounded the keyboard. Now smiling herself, she held on for support as they continued upward.

As they reached stage level, dozens more of the tiny lights switched on, shining directly onto the musicians' chairs, and, like magic, the musicians began to materialize. Jack pressed some more keys, and all the instruments floated into the hands of the players. Then the orchestra began to play.

They had barely gotten underway though before Jack pulled at the organ stops once more, switching off the lights and causing the musicians to disappear. The orchestra pit sank back down below the stage. He looked up at Sophie from the keyboard.

"Starting to get the idea?" he said. "The solar energy from the roof of the dome powers the generators down here. Come on, come on, there's much more!"

Holding out his hand to help, he guided Sophie down a spiral staircase. She held on tight as they descended in complete darkness. As her eyes adjusted, she noticed a golden glow coming from beneath a door. Upon reaching it, Jack turned the handle and led her into a room.

For the second time that day, Sophie was spellbound. The room was crammed from floor to ceiling with a collection of treasures. There were sculptures in rock and in marble, wood carvings, crystals that sparkled like diamonds and rubies. There were paintings and drawings, antique frames, sheets of colorful stained glass, stacks of

Often if she stared at the ocean long enough, she would see shapes beneath the waves, mysterious shadows, things glinting from below, reflecting the rays of the sun.

books, shelves full of photographs and old maps, and nautical navigational instruments. Further over, she saw a guitar, a saxophone, military uniforms complete with medals and ceremonial swords that must have been hundreds of years old, dueling pistols, and a hand-carved sailing ship. There was a holographic computer, a telephone with a brass receiver, pieces of driftwood, sheets of metal, a miniature steam engine, bouquets of exotic dried flowers, diving equipment . . . and much more. There were parts of the room that Sophie couldn't even see, since the only light came from the log fire that was crackling in an iron hearth. Ohhh . . . that must have been the source of the smoke she had seen from the beach.

"Welcome to my home," said Jack, making a sweeping gesture with his hand that also drew Sophie's attention to a faded sign that hung above the fireplace, which read, "Let Mystic Jack foretell your future and reveal your past."

"Is that you?" asked Sophie. Jack made a low bow. "At your service," he smiled, then sat down in one of the two chairs that faced the hearth. Suddenly Sophie realized she was cold; she sat down on the edge of the other chair, shivering lightly, waiting for the fire to warm her.

"Have you lived here long?" she asked.

"'Bout twenty years, I reckon," replied Jack, stretching out his long legs. "Though as time passes it gets harder to recall exactly," he added wistfully. "Guess I like to be alone."

Sophie smiled. She could understand that. "I like it too... sometimes, but sometimes I wish I had a really good friend."

"Ah, yes," said Jack, lapsing into silence. They both stared at the fire for a moment. Then something on the floor beside her chair caught Sophie's attention. She reached down and picked up a small photograph album.

"Go on, open it," said Jack in a gentle voice. She did. In it were pictures of a young woman with long dark hair, wide-set eyes like deep pools, and full lips turned upward into a slight smile. It was a face that seemed happy and sad at the same time.

Sophie studied the photograph awhile. "What's her name?" she asked, finally looking up.

"She was called Heipua," replied Mystic Jack quietly. "It means 'wreath of flowers' in the language of her people."

"Did you take this picture?" Sophie asked.

Jack nodded.

Seeing the gleam of tears in Jack's eyes, Sophie looked around the room for a way to change the subject. She looked again at the sign, and asked brightly, "So, do you still tell fortunes?"

Gently taking the photo album from her hands and closing it, he looked at her.

"Not any more," he said finally. "You see, I lost the inner eye."

"Oh, I see," said Sophie. She did not really understand what he meant, but she did not want to make him feel bad.

Abruptly Jack's mood changed. His blue eyes sparkled, his mouth broke into a smile. He got to his feet, pointing to the sign.

"Once I was the greatest. Mystic Jack, man of magic, man of mystery, of awesome psychic powers," he said.

Then he shrugged, thrust his hands into his pockets, and sat down.

"Oh, please tell me about it!" enthused Sophie. "I love stories about the old days."

"Surely you don't want to know about the past," he said. "It was all so long ago. You're so young and pretty, why should I bore you with my dusty old memories?"

"You won't bore me," said Sophie. Looking at him seriously, she continued. "You know, I just had to come here today."

Jack caught his breath, then sighed.

"I know. Hine-moana," he said in a whisper, as if to himself.

Sophie was puzzled, and yet excited.

"Hine-moana, the Storm Child," he repeated, looking at her. "Of all days you came today, the morning after the hurricane."

"I don't understand," said Sophie, but deep down, she did understand.

"I'm not sure I do either," said Jack. "I have a story to tell you. But first, I've got to show you something."

Without another word, he strode out of the room. Sophie followed him up the spiral staircase, retracing their steps, back into the Pleasure Dome. Holding her hand tightly in his, Jack led her outside onto the pier through another door, and all the while the sound of the word Hine-moana echoed in her ears.

Looking around at the dazzling blue of the sea and the sky, with the sea birds circling above, Jack took a deep gulp of the salty air, then walked on until they were at the very end of the pier. Waves rose and fell against the pilings below.

"What do you see?" Jack asked her.

Shading her eyes from the glare, Sophie looked at the waves. At first she didn't spot it. Then, squinting her eyes, she saw how, just yards from where they stood, the water suddenly changed color. From a sparkling turquoise it became the deepest, darkest purple.

"You see where the water suddenly gets much deeper," he explained. "Just there, beyond the end of this pier, lies the edge of a underwater cliff. It drops almost straight down to an extraordinary depth, more than five miles below the surface."

"Wow!" exclaimed Sophie. "How come they never told us in school?"

"This town has good reason to want to forget all about the ocean," replied Jack.

Suddently she heard another voice. harsh, rasping laugh was coming from the room beyond the main stairway. It used to be a sailors' bar known as The Snug.

"But why?" asked Sophie. "It's so beautiful."

"Yes, it certainly is," agreed Jack, "but the ocean is also wild and untamed, a force man cannot control."

"You see that cliff? Well, it was caused by a huge earthquake that took place at the turn of the century."

"Now I've heard of that," Sophie smiled.

"Well", said Jack, "the great quake not only destroyed every town along the shore of the Southern Sea, but it uncovered the vein of silver ore that gave Silver Mine Bay its name, but that wasn't all. The aftershock set off an enormous tidal wave, right around the planet. To this day the same wave continues to circle the globe, just as strong today as it was then."

"I've heard stories about the great wave," Sophie said, "but I never knew if they were true. So it really does exist?"

Jack nodded his head solemnly.
"Oh, yes."

Then, he led her to a door at back of the Pleasure Dome. They stepped through it into darkness. Jack fumbled for a few seconds before he found an electric lantern.

"Behold!" he cried, and pulled the tarpaulin cover off a large object in the center of the floor, revealing a steel sphere with what looked like portholes in its sides, like some sort of underwater diving bell.

Sophie stepped up for a closer look. Peering inside, she saw that there was just enough room for two people.

Everything about it was beautifully constructed and polished to a silvery sheen.

"This is really great," she said, running a hand over its smooth, brushed surface.

Jack smiled. "Took me ten years to build. Made it out of steel alloy and brass I took off the pier."

"How do you get it into the water?" Sophie asked.

"Directly from here," he replied.

Looking up, Sophie noticed a heavy winch bolted to a metal cross beam that ran from wall to wall.

"So," Sophie said, full of curiosity, "does it work? How deep can it go?" "So far, I've only tested it in shallow water, but it seems to work just fine," said Jack, still smiling. "You see, it's designed to go to the bottom of the deepest ocean in the world, which is right here, off the end of this pier."

"Wow," cried Sophie.

"Ah, but there's still one more thing I have to show you," said Jack, "before I can tell you my story."

"You see, Hine-moana – I mean, Sophie – there are two things I want to do before I leave this world."

She wanted to interrupt him, to tell him he would never leave, but he continued.

"One is to go down in my diving bell to the bottom of the undersea cliff. The other," he said, opening a trap door in the floor, "is to surf the great wave clear across the Southern Sea."

Sophie peered below and saw, suspended in the waves beneath the pier, the largest surfboard she had ever seen. It must have been forty feet long, and its polished surface gleamed through the frothing blue water beneath.

"It's made of a combination of hardwood and resin." Jack explained. "No man-made substances. In fact, I used the same materials the People of the Long Boats used when they migrated across the Great Ocean many centuries ago."

Carefully, Jack closed the trap door. They both stepped out onto the pier again and walked over to the railing. Sophie glanced up at Jack, who was silently looking out to sea. He was certainly a mysterious sort.

"Why do you want to surf the wave?" Sophie asked.

For a moment Jack did not answer. Then he turned to her and smiled. "The wave?"

She nodded.

"Well, my dear," he replied, "that's what my story's all about."

He took her by the hand, and they were about to turn away when, all of a sudden, two dolphins leaped out of the water right in front of them and then splashed back into the water, drenching them both in sea spray. Sophie could have sworn they winked at her. She looked up at Jack with a look of wonder on her face.

"Those are my friends, the Blue Boys," he said. "And now they're your friends, too."

Jack reached into his vest and took out a pocket watch, holding it in his palm so that Sophie could see it. The watch was made of silver, and was scratched and dented with age. Its rim was engraved with tiny dolphins, flying fish, and sea birds. Sophie picked it up to examine it more closely. Turning it over, she saw the back also bore a tiny engraving of a square-rigged, three-masted clipper ship. Underneath was an inscription that read, "Jack Shaye, Master Mariner."

"My great-great-great grandfather, I believe," said Jack. "His ship was the clipper Flying Cloud, two hundred thirty-five feet long, from Knights Head to Taffrail. Sailed it across the oceans of the world, he did."

Jack fumbled in another pocket, and finally drew out a brass compass. "Guided by this compass, the stars, and a prayer for good fortune," he smiled. "This was how it all began. The day I first held these ancient heirlooms in my hands, it was as if a door had suddenly been flung open. I was filled with their spirit. I felt like I was standing beneath the sails as the great ship raced with the wind across an unknown sea. That's when I discovered I had the inner eye. That I could see what others could not. That I could fore-tell the future."

Sophie looked up at him, her eyes begging him to go on.

In it was a picture of a young woman with long dark hair,
wide-set eyes like deep pools and full lips turned upward into a slight smile.

"I was a young man, full of hope. Back then, Silver Mine Bay was a very different place. In those days, it was bursting with energy. Those were the times of great prosperity, of great pride. And in times like those, men build monuments that will still remain long after they have been forgotten.

"Such men, having made their fortunes and conquered the material world, eventually want to seek a spiritual connection. They begin to talk about destiny and fate and the meaning of life. So you can just imagine how a leisurely stroll along the pier during the bright afternoons of spring and summer would not be complete without a visit to Mystic Jack. Mostly, their lives were an open book. Sometimes I saw tragedy ahead, but usually I was able to tell them what they wanted to hear.

"One day my own life changed in a way I had never expected nor foreseen. That's when I met Heipua. I still remember the moment I first saw her. The exact time of day, the feel of the sun on my back, the color of the ocean, the way the clouds were blowing across the sky. I never asked what had brought her to the pier that day, but I knew fate had a whole lot to do with it. Fate and the power of the ocean.

"Never let anyone tell you there's no such thing as love at first sight. I am living proof that it exists. Each of us always knew what the other was thinking, even if we became separated by great distances. Aside from destiny, there was something about our mutual love of the ocean that held us together. Maybe that's what brought her to me in the first place."

"But Heipua is such a strange name. Where did she come from?" asked Sophie.

"Maybe she came from the ocean itself," answered Jack. "Centuries ago, her people built the great long boats, which were canoes made from the trunks of huge trees. They navigated by the stars across the Great Ocean, following the great sea roads, the *ara moana*, and settled the islands and atolls. I guess Silver Mine Bay was once at the end of one of those roads."

"And then what happened?" said Sophie, and she could feel the excitement rising inside her like the tide.

"I remember, there was a full moon, like tonight. We saw the first albatross flying south. It was a sign the great wave was coming. Soon it would arrive, carrying with it the cool wind from the wild Antarctic Seas. We looked at each other and laughed. It was something so deep neither of us could put it in words, but at that moment we knew we were going to ride the great wave."

Jack fell silent. Sophie looked at his strong profile, the angles of his face sculpted by the wind, as if they had been hewn out of hardwood. She touched his arm.

"Tell me about the wave, Mystic Jack," she said.

"The wave," he replied after a few seconds. "It's like a wall of water, a wall nearly a hundred feet high. Imagine, there's a power on earth that can create something like that. It moves at a speed of about thirty knots, which means that once you've seen it, you know there's no way to avoid it.

"But Heipua and I were driven by a power we couldn't explain. We weren't afraid, not even for a minute. We built a giant surfboard, like the one I showed you, made from the finest hardwood, using the same methods as her people.

"Soon everything was ready. Then the morning came when the freshening wind off the ocean told us the day of the wave had come at last. A sailor pal of mine towed us in his sloop several miles out to sea where we cut the board loose on the dark blue waters. He wished us both good luck, then turned around and headed for shore as fast as he could go.

"I remember we sat becalmed for what seemed like a very long time. Then suddenly, the air turned cold. Shivering, we glanced behind us. Then we saw it. Thrilling and absolutely terrifying, it came right out of the mist, a mighty wall of water. We braced ourselves and steered the board toward the wave; it caught us.

"Leaning back into the crest, we soared across the ocean. For several hours straight we held on for dear life. Our hands and feet turned numb from the cold, our heads ached from the pounding wind. Then all at once, a gust caught the inside curl of the wave. The tip broke, and tons of water were about to come crashing down on us. Our only chance was to dive into the sea and hope we could stay under long enough for the wave to pass over us. I pulled Heipua's arm, screaming for her to jump. Then I saw that her foot was caught between the toe and ankle braces. But the next second, the massive waterfall hit us. Instantly we were thrust apart. Down, down I went, until finally I lost consciousness."

Sophie turned to look at Jack. She saw tears come to his eyes again.

"Next thing I remember was coming to," he continued, "coughing up sea water. By some miracle, I was safe. But where was Heipua? I pulled myself onto one of the pieces of our surfboard. The whole ocean was now flat, calm, and empty. And she was gone. I called her name over and over again until I was hoarse. The only other sound came from the sea birds gliding above."

It wasn't until Sophie laid a comforting hand on his arm that she realized she was crying, too. Brushing away his tears with the back of his hand, Jack tried to smile.

Their vessel was now completely surrounded with sea life. Sophie saw, in the shadows beyond, some much larger fish that seemed to be watching them.

"From that day on," he continued, "my inner eye was closed. A fishing boat picked me up, and I returned to the pier and let my spirit slowly die. From that day, too, Silver Mine Bay also started to change. The silver vein ran out. Prosperity and success ended; greed and envy took their place. Then came the great hurricane of '83, and here I am, alone."

Jack looked back toward the town. "Tide's out again," he said. "Time for you to be getting on home now before it gets dark."

Sophie looked up at him, suddenly lost for words. They walked in silence, arm in arm, the whole length of the pier. Then as he helped Sophie onto the ladder, Jack hugged her for a moment. "I'll see you tomorrow," he said gently and waved.

"Oh, by the way," he shouted after her.

Sophie turned.

"Happy birthday, Hine-moana!" he said.

"How did you know?" Sophie called out, grinning with surprise.

Jack smiled, then disappeared.

Sophie squished across the wet sand of the beach and made her way along the promenade to the hotel, full of the new excitement of her visit to Mystic Jack. Instead of heading straight for her room, she walked down the hall toward the bar.

Peeking through the door, she saw the same group as the night before, but something about them had changed. Now, seated around a circular table, they were whispering and gesturing. On the table top she could see a handful of bright pebbles that caught and reflected the light.

She strained to hear what they were saying.

"No! No!" Seamus O'Sullivan was grunting, "found 'em out on Confucius Point, washed up by the storm all right. I've never seen anything like 'em there before."

"You know what this means," said Tom Valentine.

"Yes", said her father. "It means there are silver deposits out in the bay. The seam must run much further than anyone thought. It was never completely mined out."

"We've gotta move fast," said Valentine with a sly chuckle. "There are people who'd do 'bout anything to get their hands on silver again."

"Yeah," added Seamus O'Sullivan. "And we've got to make sure it's all for us."

"Maybe we shouldn't be so hasty," said her father, but his cronies reacted with scorn. They had the gleam of silver in their eyes, and nothing was going to stop them.

Sophie made a slight movement; the men quickly turned toward the door and saw her.

"How long have you been standing there?" her father asked, surprised.

"Oh, really no time at all," replied Sophie. "I just got home."

"Come over into the light where I can see you," he told her.

Sophie stepped into the room. She felt the suspicious eyes of the men upon her. Her father seemed upset and embarrassed, torn between his friends and his daughter.

"Where have you been all day? The hotel is a mess."

Sophie took a deep breath.

"Today is my birthday," she began, "so I went for a walk on the beach. It was low tide so I climbed up onto the pier. I saw smoke and I wanted to find out where it was coming from . And out on the pier there's this man called Mystic Jack. He lives there all alone, and he's built a diving bell to explore the bottom of the ocean . . . and he told me wonderful stories about his life and about the Great Wave . . ."

"Mystic Jack Shaye! That crazy old fool?" yelled O'Sullivan.

"Just a minute," interrupted Tom Valentine, looking at Sophie.

"You say this Jack Shaye has built a diving bell?"

"Yes!" Sophie blurted out. "It's just incredible . . ."

Her words trailed off as she noticed the two men exchange an odd look.

"Bah!" her father said. "The man's just a dreamer. You

don't seriously think it would work, do you? Now, Sophie, go and get yourself some dinner in the kitchen and off to bed. You've had a big day."

A little while later, as she lay in her bed, Sophie thought of the strange looks on the faces of her father's friends, and of her father's curious reaction. It seemed as if he didn't really believe his own words. Then she remembered the snow falling in the Pleasure Dome, the leaping dolphins called the Blue Boys which had winked at her, and her new friend Mystic Jack . . . and how she loved it when he called her Storm Child.

She falls sound asleep.
Then the sun shines
and you see her smile
you see her laugh, and say,
This is my life
This is my dream
This is my world . . .to stay.

SUNDAY

THE NEXT MORNING SHE AWOKE with the dawn. Coming downstairs, she found the house empty. Quickly she ate breakfast, grabbed a sweater, and ran outside. She didn't want to miss the morning low tide.

When she finally got to the pier she found Mystic Jack, waiting to help her up the ladder.

"What does it mean to be the Storm Child?" she asked him, looking intently into his blue eyes.

"Honestly, I can't tell you yet," he replied. "But today is going to be a big day. I'm taking the diving bell down to the cliff face, and I want you to come with me."

"Oh, yes!" cried Sophie with excitement. "Will it be dangerous?" she asked after a few seconds. Suddenly she had a funny feeling as she remembered the strange look in the eyes of the men in the bar last evening.

"Not if you do exactly as I tell you," Jack smiled. "The last thing I would ever do is put you in danger. But I'm certain we were meant to do this together, as certain as I'll ever be. Whatever answers we seek, we'll find them out there, in the deep."

"I believe you," said Sophie solemnly. She felt relieved. Could it be that Mystic Jack was leading her where she had wanted to go all along?

She followed him into the loading bay and helped him attach the winch to the sleek vessel. Next Jack lifted the sections of decking beneath the diving bell. It hung there, suspended just above the waves.

"Now all we have to do is wait for the tide to come in so that the water is deep enough. In the meantime, I shall demonstrate the inner workings of my undersea craft," exclaimed Jack with a flourish.

Producing a short stepladder, he helped Sophie climb into the diving bell.

Settling herself inside, she looked around her in wonder at the complex control system with its lights and switches and digital video screens.

"You actually built all this yourself?" she asked as Jack clambered into the seat beside her.

He nodded.

"Pirated most of the computer parts from the Pleasure Dome, I did. They used to be inside two tap-dancing robot penguins. Those were some kind of smart penguins, let me tell you!" he added laughing. "I installed their control systems in here. Now they coordinate the steering and the remote arm."

"Penguins!" cried Sophie with delight. "Are you sure this will work, Mystic Jack?"

"Sure as you're born, Hine-moana. The technology is excellent. We also have an onboard air supply. With both of us in here, we should still be able to stay underwater for up to two hours."

The two dolphins rushed by, racing for the surface,
and Sophie thought she could hear their excited chatter as they shot past.

He pulled out his watch, the one engraved with the clipper ship and the dolphins, and then flipped on a video screen. On it they could see the water below from a remote camera.

"That's it, tide's in. Let's go," said Jack, and he reached across to fasten Sophie's seat belt. Standing up, he pulled the hatch closed and tightened the brass pressure bolts. Then he pressed a button on the main control panel. There was a faint whirring sound as the diving bell was slowly lowered into the water.

As they slipped beneath the surface, Jack pressed the starter, and the engines began to hum. He glanced at Sophie, and gave her hand a reassuring squeeze.

Sophie looked at him with an excited smile. How far away the empty hotel seemed now!

When the water level had closed over the portholes, Jack reached up and released the winch cable. Then they moved slowly forward, emerging from under the pier, just below the water's surface. As they went, Sophie watched his every move. "Why, I could drive this wonderful craft by myself," she thought.

Sophie turned her gaze to the undersea world, spellbound at its beauty. The visibility was amazing. Instead of fear or awe, she felt the blue water beckoning to her.

Around them, thousands – no, millions – of fish in every size and color glided by serenely. As the diving bell arrived at the edge of the undersea cliff, bright red coral reached out with delicate, slowly moving fingers, sea horses bobbed by in the wake of the giant wings of a manta ray. Blue parrotfish blinked at Sophie and kissed the porthole as they were caught in a cloud of bubbles. There were red snappers, rainbow runners, silver barracuda, goatfish, and fat, slow-moving groupers, white mullet, two-bar bream, and a shoal of darting Indian mackerel.

As they traveled deeper and the blue water darkened to indigo, Jack turned on a powerful exterior light. Their vessel was now completely surrounded with sea life. Her face pressed against the glass, Sophie saw, in the shadows beyond, some much larger fish that seemed to be watching them: blue fin tuna, wahoo, short-fin mako sharks, sword-fish, and gleaming blue marlin. The two dolphins rushed by, racing for the surface, and Sophie thought she could hear their excited chatter as they shot past.

Although they had only ventured a short distance down the cliff face, Mystic Jack decided to bring the diving bell back up. This was its first deep-water test. In fact, they had been down longer than he had realized. As they broke the surface under the pier, he registered that nearly an hour had passed. Soon the winch was attached, the diving bell was safely nestled in the loading bay, and Sophie climbed down the ladder.

What she didn't see as she left the pier and headed for

home were her father's pals Seamus O'Sullivan, Tom Valentine, and Chester Parks, who were hiding with a pair of powerful laser binoculars, spying on them behind a section of the sea wall.

"He's alone out there, after all," said O'Sullivan.

"We'll wait till the kid's gone and then we'll pay him a little visit," Valentine answered, his voice hissing.

Sophie ran home, bursting with wonder at all she had seen. She found her father alone and she blurted it all out, telling him about the fantastic fish, about Mystic Jack, and of course everything she had learned about the diving bell.

As she talked, a look of deep worry came over his face. She started to get a strange feeling in her stomach.

"Where are Mr. O'Sullivan and Mr. Valentine and Mr. Parks?" she asked him.

"I don't know," he said with a worried tone in his voice, a tone she had never heard before. "They're usually here at this hour. They will probably show up soon."

That night, as Sophie turned and tossed in her bed, Mystic Jack was awakened by a loud noise beneath his room. He heard footsteps and muffled voices. All of a sudden there was another noise, like a crash. He rushed up onto the deck. A tugboat had rammed the pier and was tied up. Worse yet, several men had broken into the loading bay and were lifting his diving bell onto the tug. In a surge of anger, Jack sprinted across the boardwalk, grabbed the nearest man, and knocked him to the deck, but quickly several others came up from behind him and struck him across the head, knocking him unconscious.

At that very instant Sophie sat up in bed. She knew immediately that something was terribly wrong. Pulling on her sweatshirt as she tiptoed downstairs, she grabbed a flashlight, then silently let herself out through the front door. Her first thought was simply to run as fast as she could to the pier. Then she had another idea.

Racing round to the back of the hotel, she pulled at the garage doors. They opened easily. Using the flashlight, she peered inside. Among the piles of broken furniture and rolls of worn-out carpet, she spotted what she was looking for, several beach gliders stacked together in a corner.

Now if they would only work! She grabbed hold of the first one, using all her strength to pull it outside. She got on and pressed the starter. Nothing happened. She bit her lip. Again, she looked carefully at the controls, trying to concentrate and not panic. Then she spotted it, the switch that read Power. She flipped it, then pressed the starter button again.

The sound of the beach glider starting up awakened her father. Getting to his feet and shaking his head, he ran over to the office window just in time to see her jump onto the

As all memory came flooding back, Sophie looked at the familiar faces, smiling perpetual smiles.

machine at the edge of the promenade.

With a low hum the glider lifted into the air. Pushing hard on the handlebars, Sophie was off. As she raced along the beach, she could already see smoke and flames rising from the pier, and the dark hulk of the tugboat moored alongside.

Fortunately, the tide was out. She jumped from the beach glider and scrambled up onto the pier deck. The tugboat was already pulling away with Mystic Jack's marvelous diving bell lashed down on its stern. On the pier an oil drum was on fire. Through the flames Sophie saw the faces of Seamus O'Sullivan, Tom Valentine the tailor, and Chester Parks on the tug. They were laughing crazily, and their faces gleamed with greed.

Sophie frantically looked for Jack. Calling his name repeatedly, she soon spotted him lying where he had been hit, beside the door to the Pleasure Dome.

"Mystic Jack! Mystic Jack", she cried as she knelt to cradle his head in her hands.

Groggily, he made an effort to stand. "The fire, the fire!" he said. "We've got to stop the fire before it spreads!"

Quickly, as if she'd been fighting fires all her life, Sophie picked up a long pole and pushed the burning oil drum into the sea. At that very second, another oil drum broke loose and came rolling across the deck straight toward her. Too late. Before she could jump out of the way it hit her hard against the legs. Losing her balance, she fell into the sea.

With his chest heaving, Sophie's father came to a stop at the edge of the promenade just in time to catch a glimpse of her small body plunging into the water. Even though he could not see clearly in the gray light of dawn, he knew it was Sophie. The tugboat was already clear of the pier and heading out toward deep water. There was no doubt in his mind: his friends would stop at nothing to get at the silver, not even his daughter.

An anger he hadn't known in years hit him like a gust of wind.

She grabbed hold of a beach glider. Pushing hard on the handlebars, Sophie was off.

The Storm Child
knows that it's true
There's nothing like love
From the stars above
To the depths of the Ocean so blue.

MONDAY

BY THEN THE MORNING SUN had just started to rise and the tide was flowing. The currents around the pier were particularly strong. Sophie was immediately sucked under water and carried out into the deep. The rush of cold around her small body brought her back quickly to her senses. She should have been terrified, but she felt no fear. It took her several minutes to realize that she had no difficulty breathing underwater either. She opened her eyes to find herself slowly descending once more among the inhabitants of the deep.

This time, though, it was the sea creatures turn to check out Sophie, each one seeming intent upon looking her over. Up above, her friends the Blue Boys tumbled about in play. Slowly she became aware of something even more extraordinary. They were trying to communicate with her! There were dozens of voices ringing inside her head. But what were they saying? She tried hard to listen. Soon a warm glow filled her body, because she understood their words.

"Believe in us," they said in their pleasant sing-song voices over and over again.

The sun was now sending down the most beautiful rays she had ever seen, banishing the shadows of the night and brightening the lovely blues and greens of the ocean. Filled with joy, Sophie beamed at all the fish darting and gliding around her.

She was experiencing something she could never have imagined, even in her most vivid dreams. It was as if a hidden memory had been unlocked, a curtain lifted. She realized she had seen it all before, not in her short twelve years, but in the dozens of lifetimes that preceded it.

"Hine-moana," the sea creatures greeted her.

"Hine-moana," she whispered in response, her heart filling.

She found it at last, the place where love would never die. Mystic Jack knew too. That was why Heipua was drawn to him, and he to her. It had been her fate to love Jack with a passion so great that for the rest of his days, he would always remember it.

The star readers who piloted the long boats had known the secret: a sacred balance was involved. One day, a Storm Child – Hine-moana – would come, and she would need a guide. No sacrifice would be too great because she was a special child. She had been chosen to return to the world because it had forgotten love. To her would be shown the source of love and life upon the earth, then she is to give back to the earth that simplest but most precious gift.

As all memory came flooding back, Sophie looked at the familiar faces, smiling perpetual smiles: there was Rata, the canoe builder, Tinirau, the man shaped like a fish;

there was Tahua, the spirit of the Ocean; there were the Whanau-puhi, the children of the wind.

Filled with wonder she continued to descend for a long time, down into the great depths, until time had no meaning, where there existed no yesterday and no tomorrow, only a serene and beautiful now.

Time was not on Sophie's side. Clasped gently between the speeding Blue Boys, she was now racing for the surface. The three burst into the sunlight, and the two glistening creatures quickly disappeared beneath the waves, leaving her alone in an empty blue ocean just beyond the pier.

She heard Mystic Jack's voice calling her. He hurried down to the landing stage and helped her out of the water. Her words tumbled out as she related everything that had happened to her. After she had finished, he hugged her very tightly. She had seen the meaning of his life; nothing had been in vain.

But as he released her, Sophie saw the anxiety in Jack's eyes.

"What is it, Mystic Jack?" she asked.

"It's those friends of your father's," he said. "They're convinced there's more silver in the rock along the cliff face and they're going to plant explosives to break them open."

Sophie's eyes widened in horror. "Oh no! They can't do that... they mustn't," she cried, bursting into tears. "It's all my fault. I told my father everything and those men overheard. I just couldn't help myself."

Mystic Jack put his hand over her mouth to stop the torrent of words, and smiled to reassure her.

"No, it's not your fault," he said gently. "But we have to stop them, because an explosion will be certain to set off another earthquake, and that would destroy the town once and for all."

"I've got to get back", said Sophie, leaping to her feet. With Jack following her, she ran up onto the pier. Before he could say a word in protest, she had already dove back into the ocean.

Underwater, she was immediately joined by the Blue Boys who held her between them as they had before, and they swept her away. Her heart sank when she saw that a powerful explosive charge had indeed been set against the cliff face. She looked at the timers that showed only ten minutes left! In desperation, she looked at the Blue Boys. Suddenly, from out of the darkness, six huge manta rays shot past them at tremendous speed on cloak-like wings.

As the minutes ticked by, Sophie looked on fearfully while they went to work. Meanwhile, Seamus O'Sullivan and Tom Valentine had just finished laying the rest of the charges from the deck of the tugboat.

Now there were only eight minutes left before

detonation. Seamus O'Sullivan yanked the wheel around and headed the tug for shore at full speed, cutting Mystic Jack's diving bell loose in his haste. It sank to the bottom in shallow water, its entrance hatch exposed.

Sophie was counting the minutes in her head. There were now just five minutes left! The Blue Boys were flying to and fro.

"Quick!" she told them. "Take me to the diving bell!"

The hatch was open. Moving as fast as she could, she climbed in and belted herself into the operator's seat. To her surprise, she knew all the controls. Switching on the motors, she steered the vessel down the cliff face, and as she did, she heard Mystic Jack's voice in her ears, urging her on, guiding her from afar.

"You can do it, Hine-moana! You can do it!"

Two minutes now. Time was running out.

She saw the detonator wires on the digital video screen. Quickly, quickly now she activated the robot arm and guided it toward the charge.

One minute left.

"Easy does it," Mystic Jack's voice echoed in her ears.

The mechanical hand closed around the detonator.

Sophie pulled back the lever steadily and held her breath.

Sparks showered over the undersea rocks, and the detonator tumbled slowly down the cliff face into the dark,

dark depths. The explosives were disarmed! Silver Mine Bay was saved.

As she steered the diving bell back toward the pier, the manta rays shot by the porthole in triumph and anger, like a single gigantic black sail, heading after the tugboat. Like a sudden tidal wave they swamped the plodding craft and pulled it down, down into the depths, and as it passed beneath the porthole she saw the wide-eyed, horror-filled faces of Seamus O'Sullivan, Tom Valentine, and Chester Parks, bubbles streaming from their open mouths.

Minutes later, Sophie climbed from the diving bell and splashed ashore. She raised her head and shielded her eyes against the glare of the sun just in time to see the Blue Boys plunge back into the surf and disappear.

She looked up and saw Mystic Jack, standing at the end of the pier, waving at her. Squinting into the sun she started to wave back. Then she noticed something else. Jack was not alone. There was a woman at his side. Sophie recognized her immediately. It was Heipua.

As if in a dream, she heard another voice calling her name. She looked back toward shore and saw a man hurrying toward her, splashing through the surf. It was her father.

"Are you all right, Sophie?" he said anxiously.

She looked up at him and smiled the widest smile he'd seen in twelve years.

"I tried to stop them, those greedy fools. They could've killed you!"

Sophie wanted to tell him what she had seen, she wanted to tell him that her name was Hine-moana, the Storm Child, but perhaps, deep down, he knew. So instead, she said, "You see, good can come even from a hurricane."

As they walked hand in hand back up the beach toward the hotel, Sophie noticed that the tide was ebbing rapidly. They shivered as suddenly the air became cooler.

They turned back toward the sea and saw it against the far horizon – the great wave. Father and daughter watched in awe as it swept majestically by. Just below the crest, poised like an arrow in the wind, rode a huge surfboard.

He leaned over and put his arm around her shoulder.

"Happy birthday, my Storm Child."

Jack had now set out on his last voyage. His destiny had been fulfilled. He would join Heipua at the last point in the upper world, where the spirit pauses before plunging into the unknown, and there they would be together for the rest of time, like closely joined atolls in an infinite ocean.

Sophie's purpose still lay ahead. The Storm Child's love had rescued her father from the depths of despair; now it would redeem Silver Mine Bay and all that lay beyond.

One great cycle had closed; another cycle was beginning.

Out in the sparkling blue waters of Silver Mine Bay, two dolphins leaped clear of the water.

The End

— Keith Cavele —

Independent producer of some twelve internationally released theatrical motion pictures,
including *The Burning*, *Split Second* and *Hawks*,
and screenwriter of *Chrome* and *For Better and For Worse*,
Keith Cavele recently wrote the screenplay of *Storm Child*
and will shortly be producing the motion picture, based on this book.
Storm Child is the first of several books he is writing under the auspices of
Tales of the 21st Century for the same publisher.

— Cathy Alexiou —

Born in Australia, Cathy Alexiou grew up in her parents' native Greece and followed in her father's footsteps, those of a sculptor and painter. As a teenager, she earned money painting backdrops and posters for student plays. Cathy moved to Montreal to study art at the University of Concordia. After graduating she began illustrating for advertising agencies and renderings for architects. For three years, she displayed her own original work, mainly architectural paintings, in the studio gallery she owned. She has since closed the gallery to allow herself more time to develop her art.

— Jean-Marc Bock —

Born in 1964, Jean-Marc Bock showed extraordinary talent from a very young age. He studied design at the Université du Québec à Montréal (UQAM). When he was twelve years old he was a finalist of the *La maison de demain* contest organized in 1972 by ONU and Unesco. He works frequently for advertising agencies and creates set designs for television. He allows us to enter a fantastic and ingenious ambiance, and his illustrations show both precision and freedom.

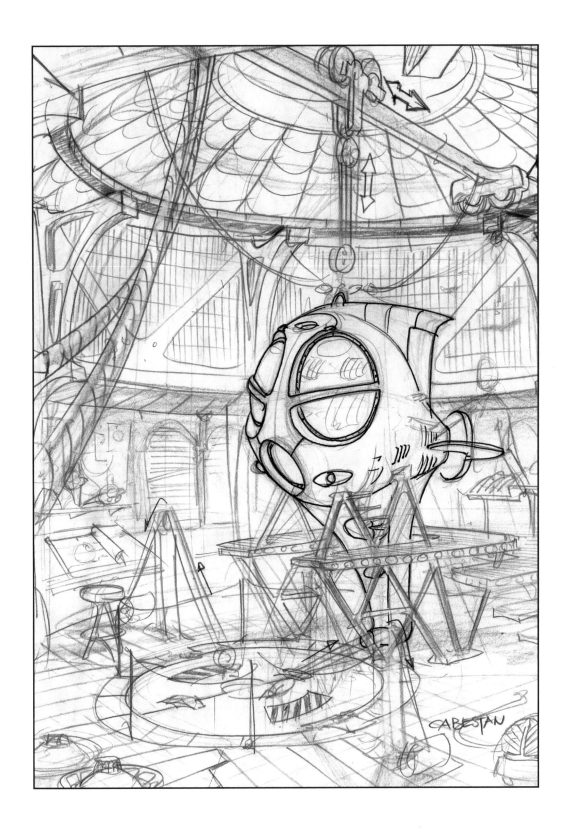

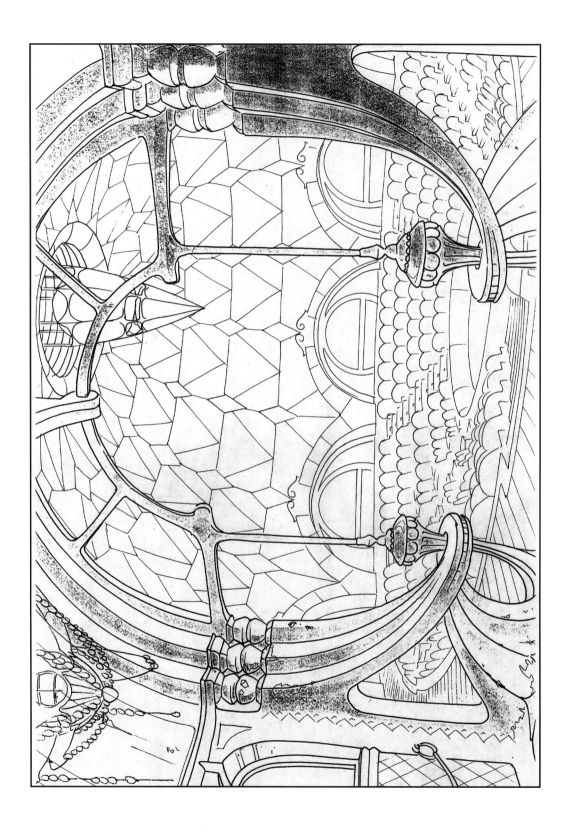

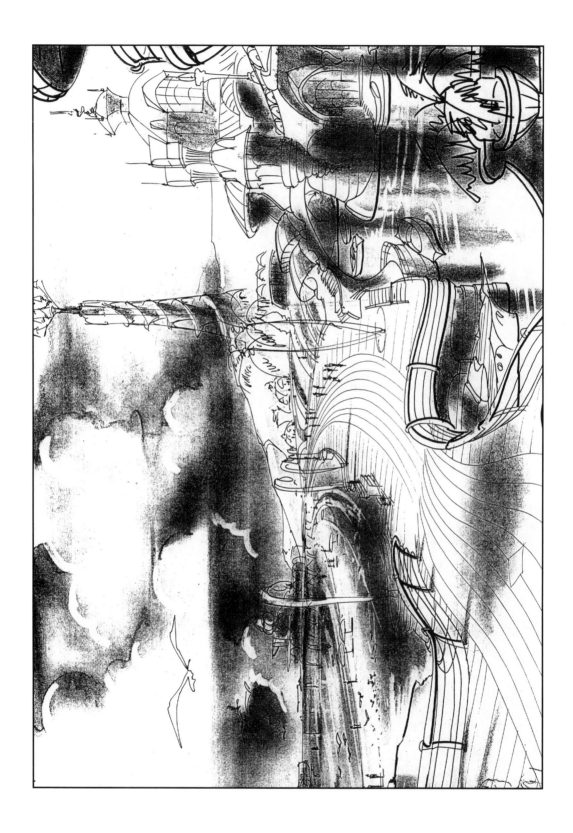

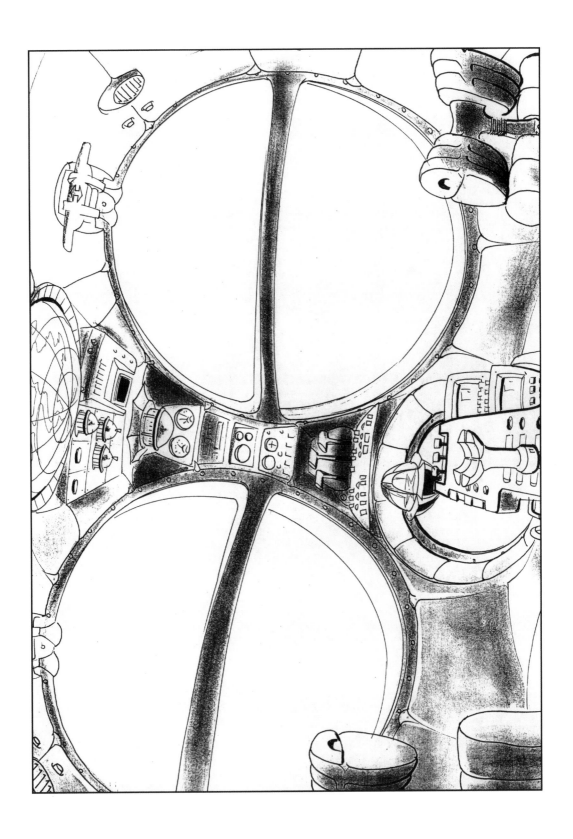

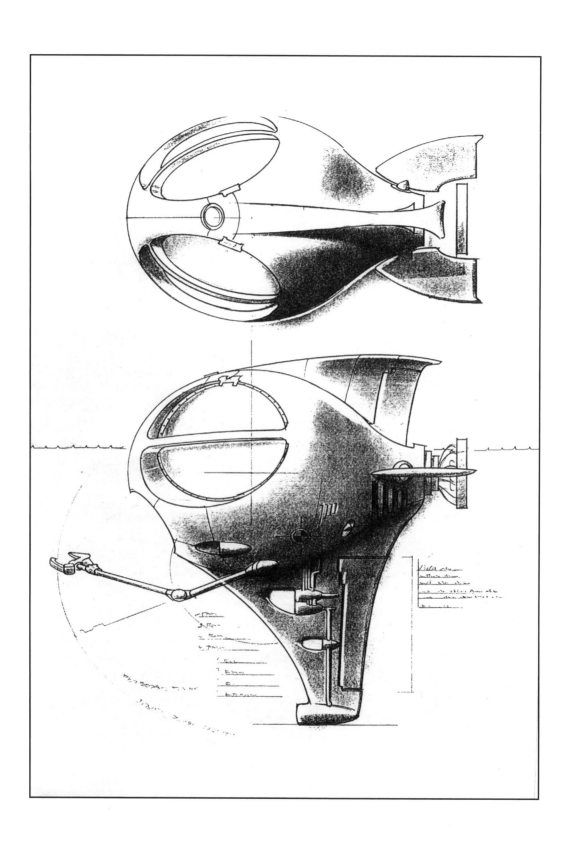

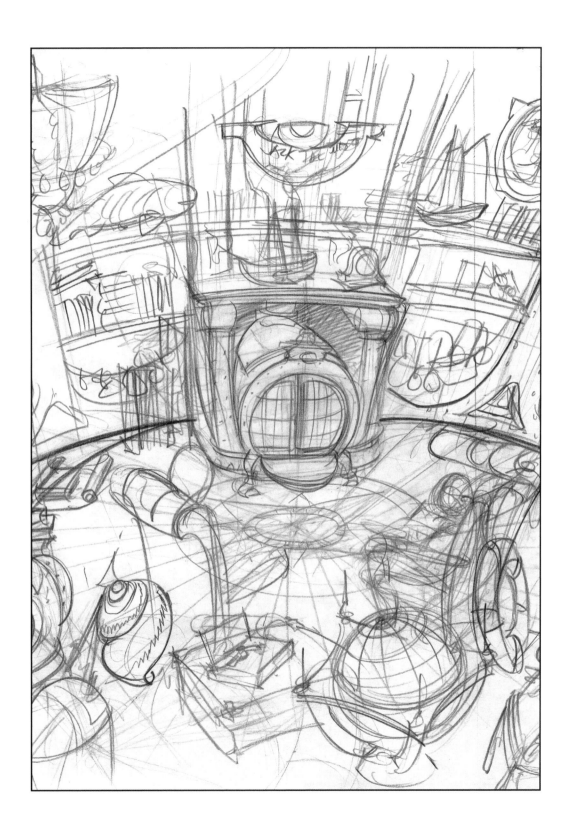